URGENT

GREENDALE

Delivery Before 9.30
Next Day Delivery
Small Packet
Sign On Delivery

On Time
12th July
Received

Sara Clifton

LOCAL POSTAGE PAID

SPECIAL DELIVERY

A special delivery by Pat and Jess · A special delivery by Pat and Jess ·

FRAGILE !

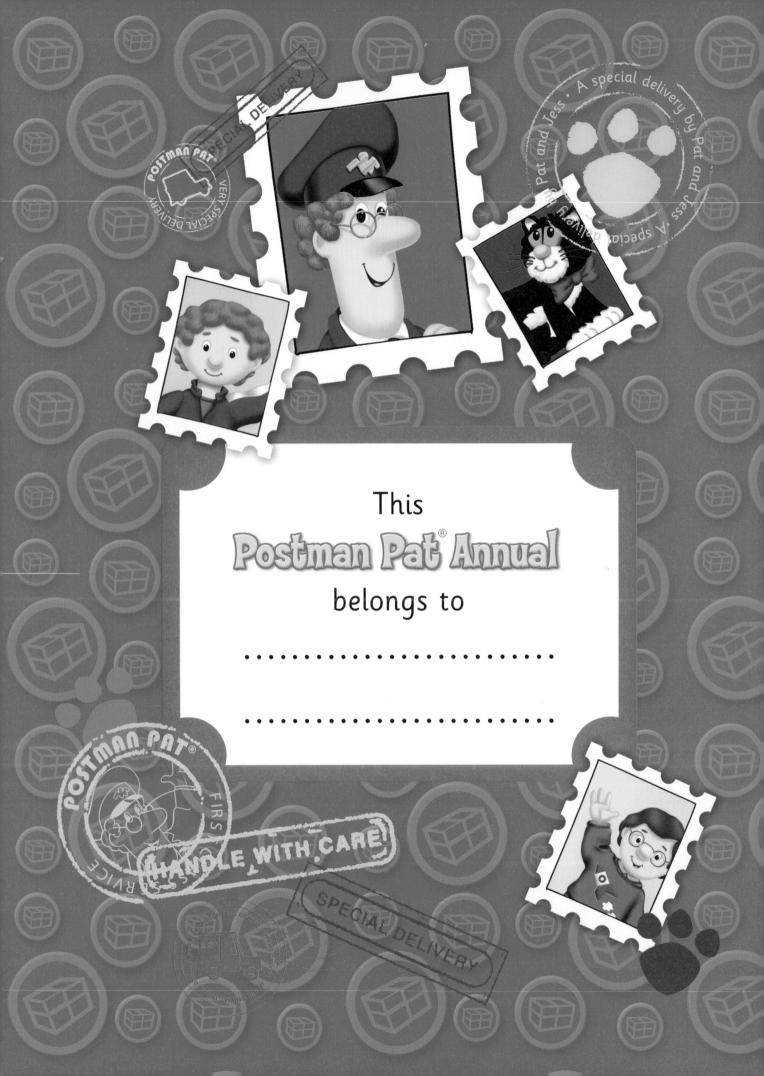

This

Postman Pat® Annual

belongs to

....

....

postman pat®

Annual 2009

Contents

URGENT

EGMONT

We bring stories to life

First published in Great Britain in 2008 by Egmont UK Limited, 239 Kensington High Street, London W8 6SA
Written and edited by Brenda Apsley; designed by Jeannette O'Toole.

Postman Pat® © 2008 Woodland Animations Ltd, a division of Entertainment Rights PLC.
Licensed by Entertainment Rights PLC. Original writer John Cunliffe. Royal Mail and Post Office imagery
is used by kind permission of Royal Mail Group PLC. All rights reserved.
Theme tune composed by Bryan Daly and arranged by Simon Woodgate™ & © Post Music (MCS).

ISBN 978 1 4052 3919 6
1 3 5 7 9 10 8 6 4 2
Printed in Italy

Postman Pat

Join in with Postman Pat's special song.
When you see a picture, sing the name or word.

Postman Pat, Postman Pat,

 and his black and white cat,

Early in the morning,

Just as day is dawning,

He picks up all the postbags in his !

Postman Pat, Postman Pat,

 and his black and white cat,

All the birds are singing,

The day is just beginning,

 feels he's a really happy man!

8

Everyone calls **Pat Clifton** Postman Pat, because he's the postman in a little village called Greendale.

POSTMAN PAT®

VERY SPECIAL DELIVERY

Postman Pat's cat, **Jess**, goes on his delivery rounds with him, sitting on the front seat of the little red Post Office van.

SPECIAL DELIVERY

A special delivery by Pat and Jess. A special delivery by Pat and Jess.

Royal ER Mail

9

Friendly Greendale

Lots of people live and work in Greendale. It's a very friendly place!

Postman Pat and his family live at Forge Cottage. Postman Pat's wife, **Sara**, is really good at baking cakes. She loves her job in the kitchen of the station café.

Postman Pat's son **Julian** is six years old and, like his dad, he loves playing football, and watching his favourite team, Pencaster United.

HANDLE WITH CARE

Postman Pat works with **Mrs Goggins**, who looks after the Post Office. She has a little white dog called **Bonnie**.

The Greendale policeman is called **PC Arthur Selby**. He sorts out the traffic and makes sure the roads are safe.

Lucy Selby is seven. She likes reading, and playing 'Let's Pretend' games.

Doctor Sylvia Gilbertson works at the Greendale health clinic.

Sarah Gilbertson is eight, and she's always asking questions!

Jeff Pringle is the teacher at Greendale Primary School.

Charlie Pringle is seven, and he loves playing games on his computer.

Reverend Peter Timms is the Greendale vicar. He lives in a house next to the church.

Friends and Neighbours

HANDLE WITH CARE

There are lots of farms in the countryside around Greendale.

Alf and **Dorothy Thompson** keep chickens, goats and sheep on their farm, Thompson Ground.

URGENT

Bill Thompson is nine, and he wants to be a farmer when he grows up.

Ted Glen, the Greendale handyman, lives at the old Watermill. He can make and mend all sorts of things, and he's full of ideas for new inventions, too!

Greendale Farm is run by **Julia Pottage**. She has lots of sheep, and a big herd of cows. You can read about them on page 16.

Tom and **Katy Pottage** are six-year-old twins. They have pet sheep called **Parsley** and **Sage**.

Amy the vet looks after all the farm animals and pets in Greendale. You can read a story about her pony, **Pumpkin**, on page 24.

The Bains Family

Ajay Bains works at the Greendale Light Railway. He drives the old steam engine, the **Greendale Rocket**, and looks after the station.

Nisha, Ajay's wife, sells tickets for the train, and serves in the station café with Sara.

Meera is seven. She likes ice skating, as you'll see when you read the story on page 58.

The baby of the Bains family is **Nikhil**, who is six months old. He's always smiling!

SPECIAL DELIVERY

POSTMAN PAT
CLASS POSTAGE PAID

Can you find the names of Postman Pat's friends and neighbours in the word square? They are spelled out across, from left to right, and down, from top to bottom.

Draw a line through each name when you find it, and tick the list.

T	A	J	P	A	M	Y
E	J	E	S	S	E	O
D	U	F	A	M	E	O
A	L	F	R	X	R	L
Y	I	S	A	J	A	Y
P	A	M	K	Q	G	I
Z	N	N	I	S	H	A

☐ **AJAY**

☐ **MEERA**

☐ **ALF**

☐ **NISHA**

☐ **AMY**

☐ **SARA**

☐ **JEFF**

☐ **TED**

☐ **JULIAN**

There's one more name to find hiding in the puzzle: **JESS!**

15

ANSWERS:

Postman Pat and the Cranky Cows

One spring morning at Greendale Farm, Julia was showing Tom and Katy her new Highland cows. They had come all the way from Scotland.

"They seem a bit poorly," said Julia. "Amy's coming to have a look at them."

Mooooooooo! said the cows.

Amy couldn't find anything wrong with the cows. "They're just a bit miserable," she said.

"I think they're bored," Katy said to Tom. "Let's do a puppet show to cheer them up."

But the cows took no notice, and turned away ...

"They don't like it," said Tom.

"I bet they'll love our skateboard tricks," said Katy.

"Yeah, watch this, cows!" said Tom. **"Ta-dah!"**

But the cows still took no notice ...

"These cows are just **cranky!**" said Katy.

Meanwhile, Postman Pat had arrived at the Watermill with a parcel for Ted.

"It's bagpipes to make my new Sheep Disperser," explained Ted. "Sheep are eating Alf and Dorothy's vegetables. This'll stop them! When the sheep come to eat this cabbage on top, they step on the bellows, and the bagpipes play. The noise will scare them away, listen!"

The bagpipes made loud screeching, wailing noises.

Waaaa! Woooo!

"**Ow**, I mean, **wow!**" said Postman Pat.

Later, Postman Pat went to Greendale Farm. Katy and Tom told him about the cows.

"They're **cranky**," said Tom.

"You're right, they don't look very happy," said Postman Pat.

Just then, they heard loud screeching and wailing noises coming from Thompson Ground, across the fields.

"That's Ted's Sheep Disperser," said Postman Pat. "He's using bagpipe music to scare the sheep away from the Thompsons' vegetables."

"Well, the noise isn't scaring our cows," said Tom.

"No," said Julia. "Look, they're moving their heads in time to the music."

That gave Postman Pat an idea. "I'm going to Thompson Ground to take a look at Ted's machine," he said. "I'll be back soon."

When Postman Pat got to Thompson Ground, the sheep weren't taking any notice of the bagpipe noises coming from Ted's Sheep Disperser.

"They're not scared at all," said Dorothy.

"I don't understand it," said Ted.

"Can I borrow your bagpipes, Ted?" asked Postman Pat.

"You can have 'em!" said Ted.
"They're useless!"

19

When a crow landed on
the bellows, they made
a loud whistling noise.

The sheep stopped, listened,
then jumped out of the
vegetable patch!

"Your invention did work
after all, Ted," said Dorothy.

"You just needed a different noise,"
said Alf.

Postman Pat went back to Greendale Farm with the bagpipes. "I think
the cows are missing their old home," he said. "Scottish music might
cheer them up."

Postman Pat took a big breath,
and started to play the bagpipes.

Waaaa!
Woooo!

Mooooooooo! said the cows, swaying their heads
from side to side.

"They look happy now, don't they?" said Katy.

Postman Pat smiled. **"Och, aye!"** he said. "Now, which tune would
you like to hear next, ladies?"

A Surprise Parcel

Postman Pat has one more parcel to deliver. It's for Julian! Can you show Postman Pat the quickest way through the maze to Forge Cottage?

START →

→ FINISH

Starting at number 1,
join the dots to see what
is in Julian's surprise parcel.
You can colour in the surprise,
if you like.

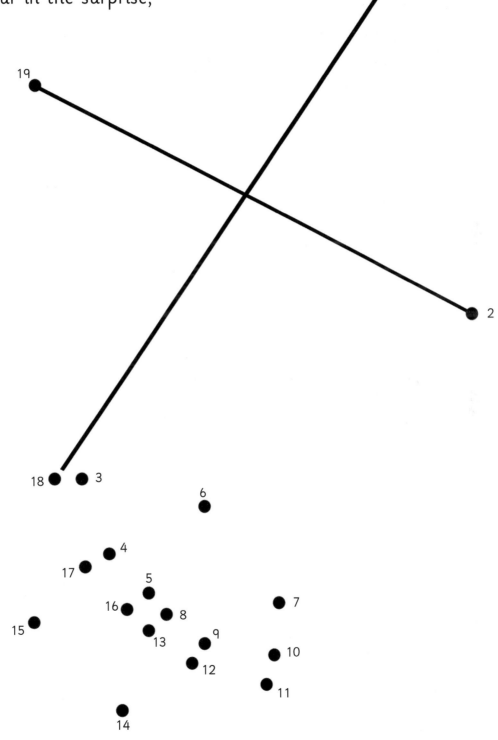

ANSWER: Julian's surprise is a kite.

Postman Pat's Big Boat Adventure

One hot, summer day, Postman Pat and Reverend Timms were helping Ted fix his boat.
But when Reverend Timms caught his foot in the rope that tied the boat to the shore, the rope came undone.

"Oh, no," said Ted. "We're drifting away from the bank! I'd better go down to the engine room and fix the engine – fast!"

Suddenly, there was a loud bang! and when Ted came back up on deck, his face was covered in grey soot.

"Are you all right, Ted?" asked Pat.

"I am," said Ted. "But the engine's not!"

"This is all my fault," said Reverend Timms. "I'll swim for help." "No!" said Postman Pat. "It's best if we stick together."

After a while, a hard wind started to blow, so Postman Pat climbed right to the top of the tall mast to unfold the sail.

But the wind suddenly dropped again, and the boat was still far away from the shore.

Then Ted had an idea. He flattened a juice carton, tied it to a mop handle to make a paddle, and used it to row back to the shore.

But the boat moved very slowly. Paddling was hard work!

At the stables, Bill, Meera and Charlie were helping Amy with her pony, Pumpkin.

"I'll top up the food and water," said Meera. "You two can do the mucking out."

"No, we should **all** help with that smelly job!" said Bill.

"No!" said Meera.

"Yes!" said Bill.

"Stop arguing, you two," said Charlie. "Let's work together."

"Now, who'd like a ride?" asked Amy, when the jobs were done.

"Me!" said Meera.

"No, me!" said Bill.

"Stop arguing, you two," said Amy. "Charlie, you can have the first ride."

Charlie rode Pumpkin to the Watermill. The others came, too.
When they got to the Watermill, Amy saw Postman Pat waving
to her from the boat.

"The engine's not working!" Pat shouted. "We can't get back!"
"Get a rope and row it out to us, then pull us in from the shore,"
said Ted.
"But how are we going to pull them?" said Charlie. "We're not
strong enough!"

"But Pumpkin is!" said Amy. "I need one of you to come with me to throw the rope, and two of you to guide Pumpkin."

"Want to go in the boat, Meera?" asked Bill.

"No, I'll help Charlie with Pumpkin," said Meera. "You go."

Amy rowed out to the boat and Bill threw one end of the rope to Postman Pat. Then they rowed back to the shore, and tied the other end of the rope to Pumpkin's reins.

Charlie led Pumpkin away from the water, and as he walked, the rope tightened, and the boat was pulled towards the shore.

Pumpkin loves apples, so he pulled really hard when Meera showed him a big juicy red one, and soon the boat was back on the shore.

"Thanks, everyone," said Postman Pat. "That was a great team effort."

"Yes," said Reverend Timms. "You're a hero, Pumpkin, and that was quite an adventure, wasn't it? **For all of us!**"

Pumpkin the Hero

"You're a hero!" said Reverend Timms when Pumpkin pulled Ted's boat back to the shore.

Look very carefully. Which of these little pictures can you see in the big picture opposite? Tick ✔ each one you find.

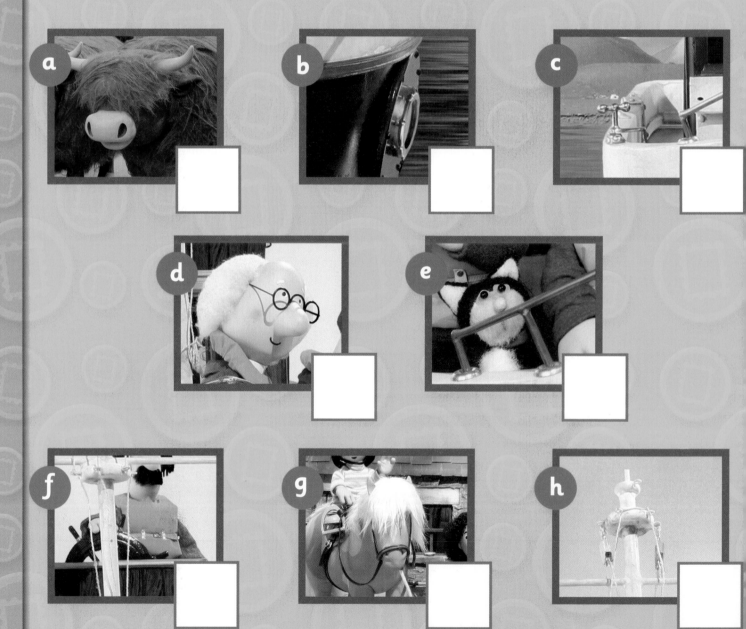

ANSWERS: b, c, d, f and h can all be found in the big picture.

Postman Pat and the Double Disguise

URGENT

A special delivery by Pat and Jess

One morning, Julia was sorting out some old clothes
for Nisha's summer jumble sale.

Katy and Tom tried to help, but they got the clothes all mixed up.

"Off you go and let me get on with the jumble," said Julia.

"Come on, Tom," said Katy. "Let's find someone else to help."

When Postman Pat went out on
his rounds, his first letter was for Alf.
But while he and Alf had a chat, they
didn't see Rosie the goat stick her head
in Postman Pat's bag, and take out
a little parcel addressed to Ajay!

32

Katy and Tom went to help Ted build some shelves, but they didn't do very well!

"Tell you what, you can help by giving this old coat to your mum for the sale," said Ted.

Next, Katy and Tom went to the station to

help Ajay mend the Rocket, but they kept passing him the wrong tools.

"Mending engines is a job for grown-ups," said Ajay. **"Off you go."**

"We should have known ..." said Tom.

When Postman Pat got to the station, he couldn't find the parcel he had for Ajay, and went back to look for it. It was the one naughty Rosie the goat had taken!

Tom and Katy were now at the stables, helping Amy.

"You can fill Pumpkin's water bucket," said Amy.

But the bucket was very heavy, and the water ended up on the ground. "Oh dear, that was a grown-up job," said Amy.

When Amy went off on her rounds, Tom looked around. He found Amy's sunglasses and her big hat,

and put them on.

"You look really grown-up, Tom!" said Katy. "Hey, I've got an idea ..."

Katy put on the big old coat Ted had given them for the jumble sale. Then she put on Amy's sunglasses and hat, and climbed on to Tom's shoulders.

"Now we look like a grown-up," said Katy. "We're big enough to help!"

Postman Pat couldn't find the special delivery parcel, so he went back to tell Ajay.

Just then, **Tom and Katy** walked into the station.

"Have you seen a small parcel, sir?" asked Ajay.

Katy nodded. She and Tom had just seen Rosie the goat dropping a parcel down a drain!

Tom and Katy led Postman Pat and Ajay to the drain, and Katy pointed.

Postman Pat and Ajay tried to put their hands down into the grid, but they were too big.

"We need help," said Postman Pat. "We need someone with smaller hands."

Katy threw off her disguise. **"We can help you!"** she said.

Katy put her hand down into the drain and pulled out the parcel.

"Thank you, Katy," said Ajay, unwrapping the parcel. "This is the part that I need to mend the Rocket."

"Well done, you two!" said Postman Pat. "But why were you wearing the disguise?"

"We wanted to help people, but everyone said we had to be grown up," said Katy.

"So we dressed up as a grown-up," said Tom.

"Well, you were very helpful today!" said Postman Pat. "And you didn't have to be big to do it, did you?"

"No, we didn't, and I like being the size I am!" said Katy.

"Me too!" said Tom.

"It's our turn to help **you** now," said Postman Pat. "We'll fold up the clothes for you."

Jess pushed his face under Amy's hat.

"Look, Jess is trying on the hat!" said Katy.

"But it's much too big for him!" said Tom.

"I don't think hats are made for cats!" laughed Postman Pat.

"Meow!" said Jess.

Sweet Dreams

When Postman Pat and Jess camped out in the tent one night, they were soon fast asleep, dreaming sweet dreams.

Draw what you think Postman Pat and Jess are dreaming about, then colour in the picture using the page opposite as a guide.

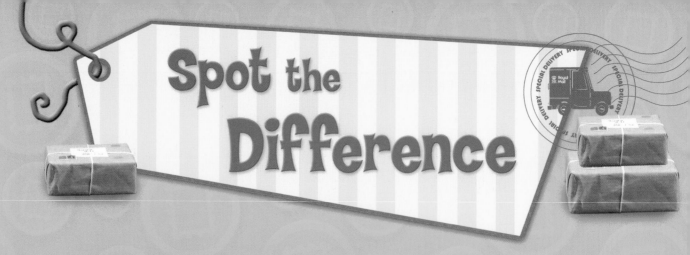

Spot the Difference

Mrs Goggins weighs all sorts of things in the Post Office shop – even her pet dog, Bonnie!

These two pictures look the same, but there are 5 things that are different in picture 2. Can you spot them all?

Postman Pat and the Fantastic Feast

One morning, Sara told Postman Pat about the famous Chef Olivier, who was going to cook some recipes at the Greendale Primary School autumn fair.

Wherever Postman Pat went that day, people were collecting things for Chef Olivier to cook.

Alf sat by the river, catching fish.

Mrs Goggins picked some cherries from the Post Office garden.

At Greendale Farm, Tom and Katy were picking carrots. "I'm faster than you!" said Katy.

"Says who?" said Tom. "Race you!"

The twins both wanted to be fastest, so they started throwing the carrots to Julia!

"Stop it, you two!" said Julia. "Come and help with the strawberry sauce instead."

In the kitchen, Tom and Katy put some strawberries into the blender. But they forgot to put the lid on, and strawberry sauce went all over everything – including Julia! SPLAT!

At the Watermill, Ted was making sausages in his new machine. He showed Postman Pat how it worked. "We pull this lever at the front," said Ted, "and sausages come out of the nozzle at the back ..."

Jess loves eating sausages, so he looked into the nozzle ... just as the sausages started to come out!

"Meow!" said Jess. In seconds he was was covered in sausages!

"Oh, heck!" said Ted.

When Postman Pat got to the school, Charlie was whisking egg whites to make meringues. "They're ready when you can tip the bowl upside down and the mixture doesn't fall out," he explained, holding the bowl over Jess' head. "Like this!"

But the mixture *did* fall out ... on to Jess!

"MEOW!" moaned Jess.

Later on, everyone arrived for Chef Olivier's cookery class. But the chef was ill, and couldn't come.

"What am I going to do with all these sausages?" said Ted.

"And my fish?" said Alf.

45

"Maybe we don't need Chef Olivier," said Postman Pat. "We can do the cooking ourselves!"
So ...

Ted cooked his **sausages**,

Julia cooked her **carrots**,

Mrs Goggins made a **cherry cake**,

Alf cooked his **fish**

and Tom and Katy made a **fruit salad**.

And this time, Charlie's meringue worked perfectly!
"Ta-dah!" smiled Pat, holding the bowl over Jess.

"What a feast!" said Postman
Pat when everything was ready.
"Let's get stuck in," said Ted.
"All that cooking's made me
really hungry!"
Jess licked his lips. "Meow!"
he purred. It was his way of saying
Can I have a sausage, please?

47

Postman Pat Saves the Day

SPECIAL DELIVERY

Can you answer these questions about the **Fantastic Feast** story?
You can use the story to help you.

1 What was the name of the chef who was coming to the autumn fair? Was it:

a. Chef Owen

b. Chef Olivier, or

c. Chef Omelette?

2 Katy and Tom helped their mum to pick peas.

True ✔ [ ]   or   **False ✗** [ ] ?

3 Which of Postman Pat's friends caught some fish?

4 What food did Ted's machine make?
Was it:

a. sausages

b. spaghetti, or

c. ice cream?

5 What kind of cake did Mrs Goggins make?

6 Who whisked egg whites and held the bowl over Jess' head? Was it:

a. Bill

b. Julian, or

c. Charlie?

7 Who made a fruit salad?

8 What did Jess want to eat?

Postman Pat and the Talking Cat

Julian was trying to find something to take
to school for Show and Tell, the next day.

"I'm taking my walkie-talkie,"
said Charlie. "It's got two handsets, so
we can talk to each other even if we're
far apart. I'll go outside and call you."

But outside, all Charlie heard were
whines and whistles. Inside, Julian didn't
hear anything at all, and went to tell
Charlie. He didn't realise that he had
dropped his handset into Jess' basket!

While Charlie fixed the walkie-talkie, Julian went back inside.
A few minutes later, he heard a voice coming from Jess' basket:
"Charlie to Julian!" the voice said. **"Charlie to Julian!"**
It looked as if Jess was talking!
Julian looked in the basket
and picked up the handset.

"Charlie," he said, "come
inside and meet the Amazing
Talking Cat!"

Charlie attached the handset
to Jess' collar and smiled. "Jess
will be the world's first **Talking
Cat**," he said. "And we'll have
the best Show and Tell ever!"

When Postman Pat started his rounds, Julian and Charlie jumped on their bikes and followed him to the church. Then Julian and Charlie hid behind a wall.

Jess sat on the wall while Postman Pat went inside.

Just then, PC Selby walked by, and Charlie said, **"Hello, Arthur!"** through his walkie-talkie in his best 'cat' voice.

"Jess?" said PC Selby.

"Meow!" said Jess.

When Postman Pat came out, PC Selby looked shocked. "Jess just spoke to me, Pat!" he said.

Postman Pat laughed. "Jess talking? I think you've been working too hard, Arthur!"

At the station, Jess ran ahead of Postman Pat and went into the kitchen. Julian and Charlie watched through the window, outside.

"Hello, Nisha!" said Charlie in his cat voice.

When Postman Pat arrived, Nisha looked shocked. "I just heard Jess talk, Pat!" she said.

"You're not the first person to play that joke on me today!" said Postman Pat. "A talking cat! Whatever next!"

At the Watermill, Postman Pat told Ted what had happened. "People keep saying Jess can talk," he said. "And talking of Jess, where is he?"

"Perhaps he got fed up of talking and went home!" said Ted. "I'll keep an eye out for him."

Back at home, Postman Pat asked if Julian and Charlie had seen Jess.

"We've not **seen** him, Dad, but we might be able to **talk** to him," said Julian.

"Eh?" said Postman Pat.

Julian showed Postman Pat the walkie-talkie, and explained that the other part was on Jess' collar.

Postman Pat spoke into the handset.

"Jess!" he called. **"Can you hear me?"**

Jess, who was exploring Ted's workshop, jumped in surprise, and Ted laughed.

"I know that voice," he said. "It's **Postman Pat**!"

Ted took the handset off Jess' collar and spoke into it. When Postman Pat heard that Jess was at the Watermill, he went to fetch him.

But when Postman Pat got back, Julian was looking miserable.

"There's no Talking Cat for Show and Tell now," he said. "We'll have to take Jess as he is."

On Show and Tell Day, it was Julian and Charlie's turn to look shocked!

"**Meow!**" said Jess to the class. "**Hello everyone!**"

"Jess, is that you?" asked Julian.

"**Yes,**" said Jess. "**I'm the Amazing Talking Cat!**"

Just then, Postman Pat came into the classroom. "**Ta-dah!**" he said. "Sorry, boys, but I couldn't resist playing a little trick on you!"

"**Meow!**" said Jess. He really was a **Talking Cat**!

Who's Talking?

Follow the wiggly line with your finger to see who Jess – the **Amazing Talking Cat!** – is talking to.

1

Jess

Tom

Charlie

Julian

Meow! Who is the **Amazing Talking Cat** talking to this time?

2

Jess

Meera

Katy

Bill

Postman Pat's Ice-capade

SPECIAL DELIVERY

One snowy winter morning, when
Postman Pat went to the station to
collect the mail, Ajay was working
on the Rocket.

"She's frozen solid," he said.
"The car park's frozen, too. How am
I going to get rid of all this ice?"

"I don't know," said Postman Pat,
going back to his van. "When I've done
my deliveries, I'll come back and give
you a hand."

But when Pat walked to his van, he slipped on the ice, and had to grab the van to stop himself falling. **"Woah!"** he said. "That was close."

Jess slipped as well, and ended up sprawled on the ice. **"Meo-oo-ow!"**

"Oh, dear!" said Postman Pat. "Today is going to be tricky!"

Julian, Bill and Meera went to the station because the school heating wasn't working, and they had been sent home.

When Meera stepped on to the icy car park, she began sliding around. "It's just like a real ice rink!" she said.

"Brilliant for sliding on!" said Bill. "Watch this! Woo-hoo! **Fantastic!**"

"Come on, Meera," said Julian. "Let's see how far you can slide!"

But Meera shook her head. "No, I want to dance like a real ice skater."

"Boring!" said Julian. "Come on, Bill, let's see who can do the best slide."

Ajay watched Meera. "You need ice skates," he said. "I've got some somewhere."

Ajay found the skates and soon he and Meera were skating. Well, Meera skated, but Ajay just wobbled and slid, and fell over a lot!

"**Ow!**" he said. "I'm going back to fixing the Rocket. It's safer!"

Postman Pat was delivering the post, when some sheep blocked the road ahead of him.

He got out of the van to move them, but the ground was so icy that he slipped and slid, then spun around, and fell down.

"**Ouch!**" he said. "This ice is making things very tricky!"

At Ted's watermill, Postman Pat slipped on the ice again, landing with another big bump.

"You need my de-icing machine," said Ted. "It melts ice in a jiffy. **Watch this!**"

Ted started the machine and pointed a tube at a pile of hard snow. "You point it at what you want to de-ice – and it melts!"

"Ajay could do with that," said Postman Pat.

Ted picked up the machine. "What are we waiting for?" he said. "**Let's go!**"

Back at the station, Ajay, Meera, Julian and Bill were drinking hot chocolate in Nisha's kitchen when Pat and Ted arrived.

By the time Ajay and the others came back outside again, the Rocket was de-iced!

"I'll de-ice the car park now," said Ted.

"No!" said Julian. "Please don't melt the ice. It's our ice rink!"

"And I want to show Mum my ice skating," said Meera. "But I need a partner. Will you skate with me, Postman Pat?"

Postman Pat smiled. "Ooohhh, go on then," he said, putting on Ajay's skates and taking Meera's hand.

Postman Pat
and Meera
twirled around ...

then Postman Pat
jumped high in
the air!

Meera skated
fast, leapt up into
the air ...

and Postman Pat
caught her!

Then Postman Pat
jumped even higher ...

and did an amazing
somersault!

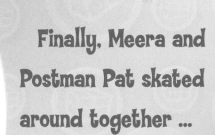

Finally, Meera and
Postman Pat skated
around together ...

then took a bow.
Ta-dah!

Ajay, Nisha, Ted, Julian and Bill clapped and cheered. They could hardly believe what they had just seen.

"Well done, Pat and Meera!" said Ajay.

"That was very impressive!" said Ted.

Pat and Meera took another bow, then skated off the ice.

"Thank you," said Postman Pat, as he suddenly wobbled, slid, and his legs went from under him! "I ... oh ... **Woah!**"

Postman Pat fell on to his back – **oof!** – and slid across the ice towards the platform, where he bumped into Jess.

"**Meow!**" cried Jess, as he flew up into the air, higher and higher. When he fell down again, he had a soft landing on ... Postman Pat!

"**Ouch!**" said Postman Pat.

"Oh, no, are you OK?" asked Meera.

"Erm, yes, thanks," said Postman Pat. "But I think I'll leave the skating to real ice dancers – like you – from now on."

"**Meow!**" said Jess. He thought that was a good idea.

A **very** good idea!

Snowballs

At the station, Julian and Bill made lots of snowballs.

"Who shall we throw them at?" said Julian.

"I know!" said Bill. "Look, over there!"

How many snowballs does **Julian** have? Tick ✔ a snowball for each one you can see. Now count them, and write the number.

◯ ◯ ◯ ◯ ◯ ◯ ◯ ◯ ◯ ◯

How many snowballs does **Bill** have? Tick ✔ a snowball for each one you can see. Now count them, and write the number.

◯ ◯ ◯ ◯ ◯ ◯ ◯ ◯ ◯ ◯

Who did Julian and Bill throw snowballs at?

Yes, it was **Ajay**, and some of them hit him!

How many snowballs have landed on Ajay? Tick ✔ a snowball for each one you can see. Now count them, and write the number.

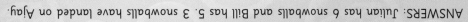

Christmas Time

Christmas is a very busy time of year for Postman Pat, because he has lots of cards and parcels to deliver.

Draw and colour in a special Christmas card for Postman Pat and Jess.

All New
Postman Pat®

Colour Me In!

OVER AN HOUR OF FESTIVE FUN!

Christmas Eve

Christmas Eve
OUT NOW ON DVD